THE GOOSE'S TALE

DEBORAH CLEARMAN

WHISPERING COYOTE PRESS

Boston

Published by Whispering Coyote Press
480 Newbury Street, Suite 104, Danvers, MA 01923
Copyright © 1996 by Deborah Clearman

Printed in Hong Kong by South China Printing Company(1988) Ltd.
10 9 8 7 6 5 4 3 2 1

Book design and production by Our House
Text was set in 14.5-point Goudy.

Library of Congress Cataloging–in–Publication Data

Clearman, Deborah, 1950–
The goose's tale / written and illustrated by Deborah Clearman.
p. cm.
Summary: One winter in a marsh near their home close to the Chesapeake Bay, a brother and sister find
a Canada goose decoy that comes to life and shares her sad story with them.
ISBN 1-879085-85-2 $15.95
[1. Canada goose—Fiction.   2. Geese—Fiction.   3. Brothers and sisters—Fiction.]   I. Title.
PZ7.C579186Go   1995
[Fic]—dc20   94-48798
CIP
AC

To my children, Sam and Tess

Winter came early. Even before Christmas, ponds had turned to ice and a dusting of snow lay on the frozen ground. Toby liked its sparkle under his boots, and the sting of still, cold air on his cheeks, as he dashed down the hill toward the river. Sunlight glinted on a ribbon of ice snaking through miles of wetland. Toby paused to yell back over his shoulder, "Come on, Liz! The marsh is frozen!"

Liz caught up with her brother at the bottom of the yard where the marsh began. Sister and brother plunged into tall reeds. The grasses rose up over their heads. Their footsteps crunched across frozen tufts of marsh. Suddenly Toby stopped and bent down to look at something.

Hidden within dense rushes was the figure of a wild goose. Its gray-brown body was made of cork, pitted with age. Its wooden head was painted black, with a patch of white under the chin reaching up behind each small yellow eye.

"It's a Canada goose decoy," Toby said. "I guess a hunter lost it."

"What a beautiful treasure! Let's take her home," Liz proposed. "We'll call her Alice."

Toby picked up the goose, and off they marched toward home.

Liz set Alice by a window in their room, looking out toward the river.

A week after Christmas the cold snap broke. Cooped up indoors, Liz and Toby watched the rain fall, melting snow and ice. The day grew dull. Bored with one game, they tried another. An argument erupted. Liz hurled a deck of cards at Toby.

"Children, stop it!" an unfamiliar voice rang out.

"Who said that?" Toby looked around, startled.

"I did. Alice."

Her beak did not move, but the eyes seemed alive in her wooden head as she gazed at the astonished children. They heard the voice again, coming from the decoy.

"Would you like to hear my story?" she asked.

The children drew near to listen. The tale began.

"Once I was a living goose, born in the far North, in a land of white nights and deep stillness, broken only by the wolf's howl and the eagle's scream. All summer I paddled on a secluded lake with my brood, while our parents watched nearby.

"In the fall we migrated. For days and weeks we flew southward, passing over rivers and forests, mountains and cities, joining other geese, thousands of us strung in long V's high above the earth.

"We came to rest for the winter on the shores of the bay you call Chesapeake. Here, we feasted on corn in broad brown fields teaming with many flocks of gabbling geese. Among them I learned of pecking order, of territory, of watching out for danger. Spring came. Again we felt the mysterious urge to migrate. I followed my family into the air to return north for another carefree summer.

"During my second winter by the Bay I noticed a young gander whose white cheeks shone like fresh snow. Our eyes met across the cornfield. A spark seemed to leap between us. He dipped his head, fluffed his feathers, and began to dance.

"Spellbound, I answered his weaving movements with movements of my own. Our necks curved toward each other. We brushed lightly together, we parted and turned, and danced again, the dance so old and so wondrously new.

"From then on White Patch and I grazed together in winter fields, and in spring we took flight together, joined for life.

"One morning last fall we took off before dawn. The approaching sunrise saturated the mist below with pink and gold. Suddenly, the leader of our string broke away in a spiralling dive. We all followed in turn, scattering through the rosy air like foam blown off a breaking wave. Eyes closed, I somersaulted through the air. When I looked again, the light of the rising sun filled my eyes. The flock was floating below on a small river. With White Patch following, I circled down to them.

"All at once a great explosion tore me out of the air and hurled me into darkness. I fell in shock and pain for a measureless time. Then the golden sun himself seemed to burn through darkness to catch me in his radiant arms. He breathed his fiery breath on me and the terrible pain subsided. He laid me down and murmured, 'Sleep!'

"When I awoke the sun was high overhead. I floated in grasses at the edge of the river, not far from the flock I had seen from the air. They were not my companions after all, but wooden geese placed by man to lure us downward. I saw White Patch beside me and tried to turn to him.

"I could not turn! My body had changed to cork and wood, like the hunter's decoys all around me. Was this what the fiery breath of my rescuer had done to me? I looked into the eyes of my mate.

"White Patch reached toward me. He stopped, and drew back his beak in confusion. He swam around me, calling our special cry. I could not answer. The hunter came and gathered his decoys, but did not see us in the tall rushes: two geese, one living and one of cork.

"Night came. And more days. White Patch stayed by my side, watching and calling forlornly.

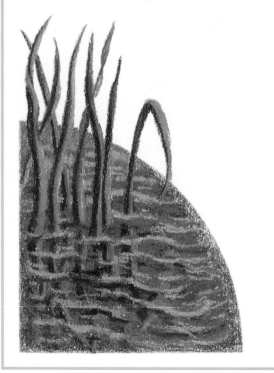

"One night a storm swept in off the Bay, lashing us with wind and icy rain and waves. I turned and swirled helplessly, pounded by waves through the night. When morning came I found myself in a marsh far up the river. White Patch was gone; I never saw him again. And there you found me, lost in a frozen world."

Silence lay thick in the room. Then Toby burst out, "Alice! Maybe we can find White Patch for you!"

"Impossible," Alice replied. "To do that you would have to fly like a goose. You and Liz are my family now, and I'll teach you all I know about the lives of wild animals."

So after school each day when the winter weather kept them in, Alice watched over Liz and Toby. They loved her stories of gosling antics and gander battles. She taught them how to hide from a coyote, where to find an updraft, and which pond weeds taste the sweetest.

Spring approached; snow melted. Green poked up through the ground and appeared on branches. Through the window Alice watched strings of her kin departing in long V's.

Their distant honking filled her with longing. The children felt it too.

"Oh, Alice!" Liz sighed. "How I wish we could fly. Can't you teach us?"

Alice promised to try.

Next morning Toby and Liz were up before dawn. Carrying Alice, they slipped out of the house and across the fields. They set the decoy down at the top of a grassy rise. The eager children listened as Alice explained the principles of flight that she had learned from countless miles of migration. As the world began to grow pink around them, the children stood poised at the top of the hill with arms outstretched.

"Go!" Toby shouted, and down they raced flapping their arms with all their strength. Faster and faster they ran and flapped, but they reached the bottom still earthbound.

"Try again!" Alice called. "Not even a gosling learns on the first try."

They trudged back up to stand again by Alice. Now as they raised their arms, a fiery arc of sun broke over the distant hills. They started to run into its blinding light.

This time the children felt a difference as they pumped their arms. Instead of wild flailing, rhythmic strokes beat powerfully against the air. Each stroke seemed to lighten their bodies, until running steps grew to leaps. With several lengthening jumps they pulled away from the earth. They cleared the treetops. Sunlight broke over them like a wave, and they pulled for the deep blue sky.

Aloft and wordless with the miracle, brother and sister turned toward each other. Instead of the familiar playmate, each saw another wild goose staring back with glittering, surprised eyes. They looked down on the world they had left behind. Alice seemed tiny, alone on her hill. They circled higher and their house grew small. The marsh opened up beyond.

Afterward, they were never sure how long the flight lasted or how far they flew. They remembered wordless ecstasy as they followed the river to the Bay. With eyes that could pick out small details from a great distance, they searched among flocks of geese awakening in quiet coves. At last they came upon a lone gander. The three flew back up the river to where Alice waited on the hill.

Riding the currents, they glided down until the hilltop came up to meet their feet. Words and laughter burst out of Toby and Liz, and they were children again.

"Alice, look! We found White Patch!"

The children watched as White Patch approached the motionless figure of his mate. He stretched out his neck, hesitated, then touched her with the tip of his bill. Slowly, Alice lifted her head and stood up on black-webbed feet. White Patch uttered a cry. Alice answered. With their necks extended, the two geese danced slowly around each other, weaving, swaying, brushing together, rustling their feathers, parting and meeting again.

Finally White Patch turned away, ran a few steps, and launched into the air. Alice gazed for a moment at the children. Her dark eyes shone with gratitude. Then she leapt into the sky, joining White Patch. Toby and Liz watched them climb until they were two tiny dots in the blue, heading north, wild and free.

Facts about Canada Geese

The Canada goose is the most familiar wild goose of North America. Many people recognize its distinctive honking as it passes high overhead.

Canada geese mate for life. They are attentive parents, and both mother and father feed, care for, and protect their young, never letting the goslings out of their sight. Their strong family ties can be maintained even after the goslings are grown and the parents are raising new goslings. Flocks are organized in a pecking order in which geese with the largest families are the most important. Canada geese are known by hunters and naturalists to be intelligent and cautious. For example, some geese act as sentries to keep watch while the rest of the flock feeds.

In the summer, Canada geese nest in northern breeding grounds from Newfoundland in the east to Alaska in the west, and as far north as the Arctic Circle. In the fall of each year, they migrate south along established routes called "flyways" to winter throughout the United States and as far south as Mexico. They then return each spring to the northern nesting grounds where they were hatched.

Extended families of geese usually return year after year to the same wintering grounds. Canada geese are, however, adaptable. They will occasionally change to a new wintering ground in response to changes in their environment affecting their food supply, the bodies of water they live near for protection, or local hunting practices.

Some geese do not migrate at all, but live year-round in temperate areas, where human presence has eliminated the goose's natural predators, creating a safe area.